Mary Norton

The Ministry of Flowers

And other Poems

Mary Norton

The Ministry of Flowers
And other Poems

ISBN/EAN: 9783744771078

Printed in Europe, USA, Canada, Australia, Japan

Cover: Foto ©Andreas Hilbeck / pixelio.de

More available books at **www.hansebooks.com**

THE MINISTRY OF FLOWERS,

AND OTHER POEMS.

Welcome Spring

THE MINISTRY OF FLOWERS

AND OTHER POEMS.

BY

MRS. Mary NORTON.

" Not useless are ye flowers, though made for pleasure,
Blooming o'er field and wave by day and night.
From every source your sanction bids me treasure
Harmless delight."
—Horace Smith.

TORONTO:

WILLIAM BRIGGS, WESLEY BUILDINGS.

Montreal: C. W. Coates.   Halifax: S. F. Huestis.

1890.

DEDICATED,

BY PERMISSION,

TO

REV. SAMUEL ROSE, D.D.,

TORONTO.

TO THE READER.

THE writer has entered the realm of thought with a poet's eye and a poet's heart. The beauties of nature for her always possessed a charm, and seemed to draw her nearer the fountain head of bliss. She has climbed the delectable mountains or wandered in flowery meads, and has here and there culled a flower whose freshness and perfume have filled her soul with delight. May she not hope that what has proved a blessing to herself may not be unacceptable to others?

In sending forth this little volume she has conquered her own timidity, strong in the conviction that she is doing right. She does not claim for it perfection, but hopes that something will be found therein which is calculated both to please and profit. She has tried to make virtue prominent, and compelled fiction to subserve her interests.

M. N.

CONTENTS.

	Page
Welcome Spring	11
Visit to a Greenhouse	14
To a Beautiful Bed of Violets	17
Composed in a Flower Garden	21
The Nasturtium	24
To a Butterfly	26
The Robins	29
Paying the Parson	32
Life in the Woods	35
The Falls of Niagara	39
Ireland, the Home of the Brave	41
Edward, of Sunnyside	45
To the Sea	49
To the Temperance Workers of Canada	51
Lines on the Death of Rev. James M. Clarke	53
The School-boys' Holiday	56
The Young Man of Excellence	59
The Coquette	61
To My Daughter, on Her Approaching Marriage	65
To My Dear and Estimable Cousin, Miss E. Blair	67
In Memoriam	70
Susan Blythe	73
On the Occasion of the Queen's Jubilee	89
Fate of the Captive Birds	90
The Lost Child	93
Aunt Phœbe's Story	96
Our Little Hattie	99
The Outlook	101
Soloma's Dream	103
Shepherds of the East	106
Beulah	108

THE MINISTRY OF FLOWERS,

AND OTHER POEMS.

WELCOME SPRING.

We welcome thee, delightful Spring,
  In sunshine or in rain;
Since thou art come a song we'll sing,
  And live our youth again.

There's many a change since last we met—
  Alternate hope and fears;
But time hath not despoiled thee yet,
  With all its woes and tears.

The earth, awaked from winter's sleep,
  Puts on her vernal dress;
And tiny pink and shoeless feet
  The green-sward lightly press.

The zephyrs, laden with perfume,
   Are stealing through the trees;
The robin pours his mellow tune
   To every passing breeze.

The wildwood flowers are peeping through
   From out their mossy bed,
All fresh and sparkling with the dew,
   Carnation, pink and red.

The maple spreads its bordered leaf
   O'er children young and gay,
Who neath its branches weave a wreath
   To crown the Queen of May.

The birds return from other lands
   To welcome thee again;
Assembled in triumphal bands,
   They sing a glad refrain.

In plumage gray they all are drest,
   They don their vernal airs,
And here decide to build their nests
   In matrimonial pairs.

The shady grove doth all invite
   To seek its sylvan bowers,
Where beauty shines with heavenly light,
   And crowns her guests with flowers.

The azure skies are smiling o'er
   New scenes of life and love ;
Earth seems a paradise once more,
   Allied to heaven above.

A thousand pleasures play their part,
   All sadness to dismiss,
And love and joy baptize the heart
   In tidal waves of bliss.

Delightful Spring, to thee we sing
   A pleasant, greeting lay ;
To thee our hearts shall fondly cling
   Till life shall pass away.

But there's beyond this shadowy vale
   A land divinely fair,
Where fount of joy shall never fail,
   And spring is ever there.

VISIT TO A GREENHOUSE.

" I loved you ever, gentle flowers,
  And made you playmates of my youth;
    The while your spirit stole
    In secret to my soul,
  To shed a softness through my ripening powers,
    And lead the thoughtful mind to deepest truth."
                                        —*R. H. Dana.*

SOFT was the radiance resting down,
  There breathed a joyous calm,
The place we trod was holy ground,
  Each lovely flower a psalm.

All bright and beautiful they stood,
  In rainbow colors drest,
And smiled upon the cold brown earth
  That clasp'd them to her breast.

The monthly roses, white and red,
  Such glory drops were they,
Like jewels hung from silken thread
  They dangled from the spray.

The lily raised its saintly head,
   The queenliest of the bower;
And over all a halo shed
   That grave, majestic flower.

Some looked a sympathetic love
   That sorrow might beguile;
Some raised their starry crown above,
   And smiled an angel's smile.

Entranced, we stood and held our breath;
   'Twas like an angel's bower;
It seemed a shrine remote from death,
   Beyond temptation's power.

And oh, to see their various forms,
   Too beautiful for earth!
Why came these lovely flowers, we ask,
   Within the range of death?

The answer, breathed from fragrant lips:
   "Our mission is divine.
We live to-day as best we may,
   And trust for coming time.

"Consider how the lilies grow,
   Which neither toil nor spin;
No heart-consuming care they know
   Their meed of life to win.

" Yet Solomon was not arrayed
    Grandly as one of these,
Which bloom in garden or in mead,
    Or 'neath the forest trees.

" Each humble flower that decks the sod,
    For gracious end was given,
Expressing well the mind of God
    To win a soul for heaven."

We felt a consecrating power,
    And lingered to admire ;
Within that temple 'twas an hour
    The soul might well desire.

TO A BEAUTIFUL BED OF VIOLETS.

BESIDE where the turncap lilies grew,
  'Neath a beautiful evergreen tree,
A bed of laughing violets blew,
  And danced to the light winds free.
'Twas there they oped their azure eyes,
  Wet with the morning dew;
They were sweet and lovely in their place,
And bent with such peculiar grace
When the dew-drops sparkled and twinkled
  On their bonnets of purple and blue.

Some looked above with glad surprise,
  And some were looking down,
And some had tear-drops in their eyes,
  And shed them on the ground.
Each had a sweet and guileless face,
  And looked so sagely wise;
But this composed their chiefest grace,
They were well adapted to their place;
Lily or rose they envy not
  Those offspring of the skies.

They peep from out their sheltery nook
    Amidst the rudest storms,
And frowning skies at length become
    Responsive to their charms.
They picture happiness and love
    Through all the changeful hours;
Of pride they bid us to beware,
And for the lowly have a care.
And thus they lead our minds above,
    These quaint, wee, bonny flowers.

We joy to meet them in the woods
    Or by the sparkling rills,
Where nature in her wilder moods
    The graver passions thrills;
For there in deeper solitude
    Their ministry we prove.
We study in their earnest eyes
The beauty of their quiet lives,
In lanes, in gardens, or in woods,
    These pleasant flowers we love.

They grow where the earth is moist and rank,
    When the buds are on the trees;
When wild flowers smile round the old sugar
        camp
    They peep through the brush and the leaves.
They bloom by the mansion or by the cot,
    By the brook with gentle flow;

They bloom in September, they bloom in May,
Looking happy and cheerful every day,
And the lesson they teach is food for thought
   While the seasons come and go.

There are three beautiful colors—
   Like velvet and satin and silk—
   One is purple, one is blue, and one is white
     as milk.
Blow, violets, near our cottage home,
   Right welcome you shall be,
Whether of dark and sombre hue,
Of yellow, white, or azure blue,
A kindly thought we'll give to you
   Where'er our lot may be.

We like the pale blue violets best,
   And such are some of ours;
Young April wears them on her breast,
   Love's emblematic flowers,
So like the sky their azure hue,
So beautiful, yet modest, too,
Like persons of superior sense
   In contrast with the vain,
Who covet not pre-eminence,
   But wisely yield the same.

Sweet, modest, unassuming flowers,
　　In you we fondly trace
The virtues of departed ones,
　　Humility and grace.
Those guardians of the wayward heart,
　　We learn to prize them so,
For, like the violets we pass,
　　Decay is sure but slow,
And soon shall bend the waving grass
　　O'er heads that slumber low.

We love the fragrant hyacinth,
　　The verbena, flowering low,
The daisy and the bridal rose
　　That blossom white as snow;
The primrose and the jessamine,
　　And the bluebells when they blow.
But without the violets, plain and neat,
The garden would be incomplete;
'Twere sad to miss their faces sweet,
　　Like the friends of long ago.

COMPOSED IN A FLOWER GARDEN.

"Your voiceless lips, O flowers! are living preachers—
    Each cup a pulpit, and each leaf a book,
Supplying to my fancy numerous teachers
      From loneliest nook.
Floral apostles! that in dewy splendor,
  'Weep without woe and blush without a crime,'
Oh, may I deeply learn, and ne'er surrender,
    Your lore sublime!"
                —Horace Smith.

I SIT 'neath this beautiful shade-tree,
  Where the sweetest and fairest of flowers,
Like a halo of glory, surround me,
  And a wide-spreading maple embowers.

Here the lilies and dahlias and fuchsias
  With more delicate flowers combine
To charm, with their fragrance and beauty,
  Like the spell of a musical chime.

Here are bluebells, all tender and tearful,
  Primula and Oscar Wild,
And daisies, that look even cheerful
  When pressed in the lap of a child.

Portulaca, befitting its station,
  The pride of the bower to-day;
And elegans, pink and carnation,
  That bend to the Zephyrs in play.

Convolvulus, coleus, peony,
  Othonna and happy thought;
And vinca, verbena, begonia,
  With lovers' forget-me-not.

Begonia rex, aster, lantana,
  And roses whose petals hang down;
Chrysanthemum, stock, oleander,
  Like jewels surmounting a crown.

Hydrangea, digitalis, oxalis,
  And others whose names I forget;
But 'tis graceful in cot or in palace,
  My sweet little love, mignonette.

Like the glorious rainbow they blended
  Their hues in the light of the sun;
But a shower of hailstones descended,
  And their grace and their beauty were gone.

To me 'twas an evident token
  That friendship and beauty and love,
Like the cords of a harp that is broken,
  Dissevered and worthless may prove.

Beyond this cold world there's a region
  Where beauty shall blossom forever ;
Removed from all blight and contagion,
  The amaranth wither shall never.

THE NASTURTIUM.

THIS sweet nasturtium large hath grown;
   'Tis crowned with blossoms, too,
All laughing in the midday sun,
   Or weeping in the dew.

The choicest in my garden row,
   A lady gave it me;
She kindly gave me one, e'en though
   In all she had but three.

We placed it here with thought and care,
   A tiny plant in June;
'Twas sheltered from the frosty air
   And scorching heat of noon.

Its growth was constant—slow but sure;
   'Twas watered morn and eve;
At length a dainty yellow flower
   Peep'd from behind the leaves.

This pretty annual comes to cheer
   And deck our humble cot—
A sweet and tender souvenir
   Of days we ne'er forgot.

When I a girl of summers ten
   Sported in childish glee,
It was my mother's favorite then
   As now it is with me.

The dew-drops from its leaves distill'd
   Might love to linger there;
Its golden cups with fragrance fill'd
   Pour incense on the air.

It speaks in language all its own—
   Soft, soothing and sublime—
Of heavenly rest and bliss to come
   Beyond the ills of time,

Where flowers of beauty, love and truth,
   That pass from earthly strife,
Shall blossom in immortal youth
   Beside the fount of life.

Thou precious flower, exceeding fair,
   Thou dost our hearts attune
To higher joys, thou beauty rare,
   And must we part so soon?

But others from thy seed shall grow
   To fill thy vacant room,
When balmy spring again shall glow
   With beauty and with bloom.

TO A BUTTERFLY.

WHY camest thou hither, butterfly,
    Invoking me a song to sing?
For soon as thou to me didst fly
    My spirit rose upon the wing;
And sing a cheerful song I will,
The melody some heart may thrill.

You fluttered in beneath the sash,
    A thing so joyous, light and free,
Then with a flourish and a flash
    You fly across the room to me,
And hover gently near my face
As if to ask a moment's grace.

And this is what you seem to say,
    You fairylike, coquettish thing:
"I stole away from playmates gay
    A ray of sunshine thee to bring."
Inspirited I grasp the pen
And write you are immortal then,

You call me back to other scenes,
　　And wake the songs of earlier years,
When childhood dreamt its golden dreams
　　Which alternate 'twixt hopes and fears;
I was whate'er I wished to be,
For mind an empire was to me.

'Tis true you spend your brightest day
　　In gossiping from flower to flower—
A round of pleasure and display,
　　A would-be queen without a dower.
In this we may not vie with you,
For life hath nobler work to do.

Yet still I like your pleasant ways;
　　Thou art a joyous thing to me,
And many a time on summer days
　　I loved to chase thee o'er the lea
With hat in hand or none at all,
Content could I but thee enthrall.

Onward I sped with courage bold
　　To seize the prize divinely fair;
But like the fabled cup of old,
　　You were not here, you were not there—
Now far away, and now so near,
Inspiring hope, exciting fear.

And oh, how often in the chase
  I longed for wings as light as air ;
For feet were cumbrous in the race,
  And loss of thee was hard to bear.
The child-heart disappointment wrings,
Then mothers give them pleasant things.

Say, have you but a generous thought ?
  To voice that thought will give it wings ;
It may be with a life inwrought,
  It may be of life's little things.
But cage it still, and lo, it dies,
The beauteous bird of paradise.

And you who, like the butterfly,
  Are happy, cheerful, young and gay,
Give loving words and pleasant smiles
  To those around you every day.
Where'er these humble virtues shine
They're sure to make the life sublime.

THE ROBINS.

[A pair of robins, evidently the same, which built their nest con-
venient to the parsonage for several successive seasons.]

A PAIR of red robins came year after year,
Making friendly excursions and bringing good cheer,
They followed the gardener, picking up worms,
And gathered material for building by turns.
Their nest in the plum-tree, conveniently high,
Held eggs that were oval and blue as the sky.
Here they nourished their young ones, and brought
  them up well,
But were they all happy the sequel shall tell.
Their mother had said, in her pleasantest mood,
"Good-bye, my dear children ; be gentle and good
When your parents are absent providing you food."

But one of the birdlings, the oldest of three—
Precocious young skipjack and upstart was he—
Assuming the air of an orator bred,
He rose in the nest with the shell on his head.

The beautiful branches that spring interweaves
Bent gracefully o'er him their emerald leaves;
His fancy took flight; he was plump and well fed,
So he rose to his height with the shell on his head;
And there, like a parson, he essayed to preach,
But only rebellion and discord to teach.
He balanced awhile on the edge of the nest,
And thus his dear brothers he roughly addrest:
" I cannot live here, in this ugly old stub,
And eat for my dinner a snail or a grub;
I'm crowded and squeezed from morning till night;
Our home is the meanest and nothing is right.
Arise! my young brothers, and come away too,
And together we'll soar to the mountains so blue."
Then each of his brothers shook gravely his head,
But never replied to a word that he said.

" Then, fare ye well, youngsters; the morning is bright,
I am off for the regions of beauty and light;
In the nest you may dwell, but the world is for me—"
Then down went the shell, and our hero was free.
Then down from the nest he made awkward descent,
And with him the spirit of proud discontent;
He fluttered an instant, then fell to the ground,
But nothing of comfort was there to be found.
He was free as the wind, the callow young dude,
But where could he find either shelter or food?
He'd gladly return to the nest in the tree,
For helpless and hopeless and hungry was he.

His eyes were like rubies, his breast was like gold,
But how shall we tell what remains to be told?
For there, in the shadow, a luckless old hen
Emerged from the clover with chicks nine or ten ;
And her long-pointed bill was as sharp as a pen,—
She flew on the birdling and shattered its wing ;
It cried and it struggled, that hapless young thing.
Friends ran to the rescue and caught up the bird,
Whose importunate wailing their bosoms had stirred ;
They applied some restoratives gently and soon,
But, alas ! for the birdling, it sank in a swoon.
Then tenderly, sadly, we laid it away ;
But I know it expired in less than a day.
Now, all you miscreants who languish to roam,
I tell you in friendship, there's no place like home.

PAYING THE PARSON.

ONCE on a time a few were met
   To hear the words of life;
But some had come to fume and fret,
   And worldliness was rife.

The parson was a forceful man,
   And well expressed his mind,
A better bred, or poorer fed,
   'Twere difficult to find.

The way to heaven, the narrow way,
   He taught them many a time;
Likewise their dues and debts to pay,
   The precept is divine.

He counselled all to be exact,
   Yet ready to forgive;
And also taught the stubborn fact,
   That men must eat to live.

A patriot of rank and blood,
   But yet an humble scholar,
Forthwith his purse-strings slow undid,
   And brought his mighty dollar.

The worthy parson quick replied,
  "Friend, this is very small;
You know I do not wish to chide,
  But let me live at all."

The patriot snuffed and cleared his throat,
  His face grew mighty red;
Essaying to excuse his groat,
  He blundered forth. instead

A tale of poverty and woe,
  And strung to this his losses,—
In other circles he would boast
  Of money and of horses.

The faithful, in dissenting mood,
  Now hum at his disgrace:
"Come, pay the parson as you should,
  Or leave this holy place.

"We want no misers in our ranks
  To shame us now and then;
No mean, dishonest, worldly cranks,
  But upright, honest men.

"For such, assembled with the good,
  Would prove a sure disgrace;
So pay the parson as you should,
  Or leave this holy place."

LIFE IN THE WOODS.

FOND memory lingers near it still,
   Though friends have passed away;
The dear old homestead on the hill
   I love, and will for aye.

Where, seated round the fire at night,
   Parents and children all,
The pine-knot lent its blazing light,
   Which flickered on the wall.

The farmer early sows the seed
   And tills the fruitful ground;
A just reward shall be his meed,
   With richest blessings crowned.

The farmer's wife she is a gem
   Whose name must be enrolled;
The mother of heroic men,
   And worth her weight in gold.

Rich freighted, like the merchant ships,
   With precious things in store,
The law of kindness in her lips,
   The patron of the poor.

Her daughters rise and call her blest,
    Among the maiden throng;
She taught them the divine behest,
    She taught them right from wrong.

Now take a maxim while you may,
    And learn it well and soon,—
Work while you work, play while you play,
    But rest yourself at noon.

But, hark! the harvesters are come
    In armor all complete;
All marching with a cheery hum
    To cut and bind the wheat.

The children play among the stacks,
    Till pleasure seems a pain;
Then come the groaning waggon racks
    With loads of precious grain.

The chickens—downy little things—
    Would lag behind the gate;
The mother spreads her sheltering wings,
    And calls, "Too late! too late!"

A friendly visit must be paid,
    To-morrow, we decide;
The wool is spun, the garments made,
    The apples peeled and dried.

Fat is the goose for Christmas use,
    The jellies golden brown ;
The eggs are packed for winter use,
    The small end always down.

'Tis hurry now, through thick and thin,
    Before the coming storm,
Les pommes de terre to gather in,
    The pumpkins and the corn.

Home come the patient, meek-eyed cows,
    Before the close of day;
The milk-pails stand in even rows
    In close and proud array.

And here no coward part is played,
    Or sought as an excuse;
The golden butter must be made
    For home and foreign use.

To market goes the precious hoard,
    The gauger goes his rounds ;
Each tub first quality is scored,
    And weighs a hundred pounds.

The buyer comes with lordly purse,
    And pays the farmer down ;
'Tis well-earned money, true and just,
    As ever came from town.

I visit, in a waking dream,
　The home of by-gone years;
Though time and distance come between,
　Yet short the time appears.

I speak into those chambers old,
　But hear no welcome voice;
Their light is dim, their breath is cold,
　I sorrow and rejoice.

For some have entered into rest,
　And some are far away;
Yet show me still the old dove nest
　I love, and will for aye.

THE FALLS OF NIAGARA.

I STAND o'erawed, as in God's nearer presence,
And contemplate with quivering, bated breath,
This awful symbol of Thy power divine,
Who madest the world and all things therein are.
Great cataract! young in thy strength and pride,
Can tongue or pen of mortal thee describe?
Like a great general, leading forth his armies
In mighty phalanx, conquering and to conquer.
Thy foaming waters, rushing wildly bland,
Were meted in the hollow of God's hand.
He sent thee forth, a proof of heaven's might,
To punish evil and protect the right;
Whose raging caldron biddest men beware,
For heaven's fixed law we mortals may not dare.
Thy rush and roar is as the din of war,
Of mighty warriors mustering near and far.
Above the vortex smooth thy current flows,—
A mighty depth, concealing mightier woes,
O'er which the frail canoe, resistless borne,
Is hurried onward; never to return.

Thou king of waters! whose impetuous sway
No barrier owns, no human laws obey!
Thou dost proclaim in thunder tones to man,
To everything a purpose, time and plan.
But who shall look with dauntless heart on thee
Till stars shall pale and time shall cease to be?
Thou art the offspring of infinite power!
Yet He who made thee made the little flower
That sweetly pours its fragrance on the air,
Because the world's Creator placed it there.

IRELAND, THE HOME OF THE BRAVE.

THE REMINDER.

DEAR Emerald Isle! all hail to thee,
  Where first I drew my breath;
To thee, my native land, I'd be
  True—faithful unto death.

O sweetest island of the sea!
  Beautiful Emerald Isle!
Sweet is thy song-birds' minstrelsy,
  And sweet thy roses' smile.

Thy daughters, fairest of the fair;
  Thy sons are gallant, brave,
The noble-hearted everywhere,
  Upon the land or wave.

Where hedgerows wear their mantles green,
  Or blossoms white as snow,
And singing-birds of every sheen
  Are flitting to and fro.

Where boxwood, palm and heather bell
    In rich profusion grow;
The laurel, yes, I mind it well,
    The hawthorn and the sloe.

Sweet Erin Isle! where roses smile,
    Where heroes fought and bled,—
Ye keep in trust the precious dust
    Of the poor but pious dead.

Why art thou still debased, oppressed,
    Afflicted and misled?
And why unheeded in the streets
    Thy children cry for bread?

Why, brothers, will you fight and kill?
    It is your country's shame;
Rum, gin and brandy made you ill,
    But yet you drink again.

The men who court politic fame
    Have robbed thee of thy might;
A hopeless warfare to maintain—
    The wrong against the right.

They drain thy coffers year by year,
    But give you naught instead;
When corn is scarce, the meal is dear,
    And children cry for bread.

The fires of discontent are fed
　By those who shun the light;
And mobs of lawless ones are led
　To crimes as black as night.

Why wilt thou still provoke high heaven
　To scourge thee yet again,—
Like Sodom and Gomorrah even,
　Those cities of the plain ?

But turn again, nor wander far,
　Muse of the starry morn;
Another thought for Ireland,
　The land where thou wast born.

Ye pious poor, who eat your bread
　With many a bursting sigh,
Rejoice, rejoice! lift up your head,
　Your refuge is on high !

Strong is the God in whom ye trust,
　Then sing a joyful psalm;
Your wily foes shall lick the dust,
　When you shall bear the palm.

When love is cherished in the home,
　And peace and joy restored,
Thou shalt, as Eden, then become
　The garden of the Lord !

To work, to work! nor idle stand,
  The vineyard waits around;
And soon the labor of your hands
  Shall be with plenty crowned.

Thy flocks and herds shall then increase,
  And fruitful be the ground;
And great shall be thy children's peace
  If righteousness abound.

Now he who would oppress the weak
  Or do them wilful wrong,
Shall not inherit what he seeks,
  Shall not his days prolong.

Remember still the Golden Rule
  Is to be kind and true;
And do to others as you would
  That others do to you.

EDWARD, OF SUNNYSIDE.

PROUD fancy tells the artless youth
  That distant hills are green;
But time reveals the startling truth,
  Things are not what they seem.

Resolved a seaman to become
  He quits his native shore,
And leaves behind his rural home
  Some region to explore.

The vessel flies before the breeze
  With canvas all unfurled;
He has resolved to plough the seas
  And sail around the world.

Yet must his friends with patience wait,
  With hope and trembling joy,
To learn the fortune or the fate
  Of this ambitious boy.

He recks not there are breaking hearts,
  Nor aught that may betide;
The stately vessel o'er the waves
  Is sporting far and wide.

But oft sad disappointment comes
  Our cherished hopes to mock ;
The freighted vessel she has run
  Against a sunken rock.

He hoped to reach a foreign land,
  And win some laurels too ;
But hope, that waved her magic wand,
  Has vanished from his view.

Dread dissolution now he sees,
  His boasted courage fails,
And the noble ship that to the breeze
  . Had spread her gallant sails ·

No human effort now can save ;
  The waves are mountains high ;
She reels, she shudders, plunges down
  Beneath an angry sky.

He struggles with the boisterous main,
  Unaided and distressed ;
A thousand fancies fire his brain,
  And terror fills his breast.

Does fate decree our hero brave
  Amongst the drowned shall sleep ;
And must he lie beneath the wave
  Full many a fathom deep ?

The voice that calms the raging sea
  When tempests rave around,

Hath bidden him live, and even he,
  Though lost, shall yet be found.

He rose, as by divine command,
  And caught a broken spar,
Which drifted him upon the strand
  With a poor but honest tar.

They hoist a signal of distress,
  'Tis but a handkerchief,
Yet doubtful if a ship ere death
  Shall come to their relief.

The moon withdrew her silver ray,
  'Tis night without a star ;
" Is heaven so very far away?"
  Thus spake the honest tar.

'Tis morn again, and on the main
  A cruiser now is seen,
Which bore away at break of day
  The hero of our dream.

And now we find him homeward bound,
  He's reached fair Sunnyside,
And hails with cheer the friends so dear,
  And her, his future bride.

He wed her at the altar soon,
  Then sought his cottage home,
To spend a quiet honeymoon
  And never more to roam.

"Thou bearest on thy bosom, amidst the strife and roar,
The gallant stately vessel safe to the distant shore."

Page 42.

TO THE SEA.

O INFINITE Creator! Thou by Thy works art known,
Eternal Legislator, who spake and it was done;
When finished was creation, Thyself pronounced it
    good,
A wondrous combination of earth and sea and flood.
Thou, who hast formed the ocean, and circled it around,
Canst calm its wild commotion and sound its depths
    profound.
O wondrous world of waters, thy chambers submarine
Have treasure for our daughters, have jewels for our
    queen;
Thou bearest on thy bosom, amidst the strife and roar,
The gallant stately vessel safe to the distant shore.
But thou hast tears, old ocean, from many a crystal
    eye,
And sad and sacred memories, such as can never die.
A loved and loving brother, whose heart beat fond and
    free
With thoughts of home and mother, hath found a grave
    in thee;

A fair and gentle sister with thy wild waves hath
        striven,
Winds heard her dying whispers and bore her sighs to
        heaven.
O'er many a priceless treasure thy billows roll with
        glee,
And wealth and gold ill gotten oft sink beneath the
        sea.
The mortal who defies thee shall to thy depths be
        hurled,
For terror underlies thee, thou world within a world.
The voice of God is in thee, though oft to man un-
        known,
It speaks in awful grandeur or solemn undertone;
It says the time is coming when thou shalt cease to be,
The loved and lost restoring, there shall be no more sea.

TO THE TEMPERANCE WORKERS OF CANADA.

Ye men of might throughout the land,
  In this momentous hour,
United stand, a valiant band,
  To crush an evil power.

Intemperance, with triple crown—
  Guilt, horror, desolation—
Is fighting still to batter down
  The bulwarks of the nation.

She asks for absolute control,
  Impassioned and impassive ;
She seeks to make the free-born soul
  Her base but willing captive.

The wine exhales its poisonous breath,
  And every fool and scoffer
Will drink and run the way of death,
  Like oxen to the slaughter.

Intemperance, that baneful tree,
  Which yields the fruit of sorrow;
The fruit of direful misery,
  With every coming morrow.

Oh, cut this deadly upas down!
  And health shall wave her pinion
O'er every hamlet, every town,
  Throughout this wide Dominion.

You say, We come to storm the fort—
  To break the drunkard's fetters;
Too long, too long we've been the sport
  Of rum and its abettors.

We act upon the Gospel plan—
  Of mercy to another;
And thus we come to rescue man,
  Who is our fallen brother.

Then, on to victory, hearts of flame;
  While you are pressing onward,
Heroic men, of every name,
  Are rushing to your standard.

The nation's foe must be laid low,
  Or woe to her condition;
God speed the right, with matchless might,
  And aid your glorious mission!

LINES

ON THE DEATH OF REV. JAMES M. CLARKE.

BEYOND the range of death he flies,
　　While friends his exit mourn,
His ransomed spirit mounts the skies,
　　Nor wishes to return.

With harp in hand he joins the band
　　Of choristers above;
The angel choirs now strike the lyre,
　　And shout redeeming love.

True wisdom early shed her light
　　On his expanding mind;
But soon he took his upward flight,
　　And left the world behind.

When death's cold hand had sealed his eyes,
　　No bell rang muffled peals;
He soared above the reach of sighs,
　　Where Christ Himself reveals,

Who binds a wreath upon the brow
   Of her he called his own;
His ardent, freed affections now
   Revolve around the throne.

Weep not for him, but let the tear
   Back to its source return;
Ere long the friends he held so dear
   Shall reach that happy bourne.

I view an Eden bright beyond
   The boundaries of time;
This deathless gem would burst its bonds
   To reach that happy clime.

No chilling tempest rudely blows
   O'er Eden's blissful bowers;
'Tis there the tree of knowledge grows,
   And amaranthine flowers.

He left his tenement of clay
   For bliss beyond the tomb;
We long to see the happy day
   When death shall meet his doom.

He rests not in a land like this,—
   Now sovereign grace he sings;
He drinks the flowing streams of bliss,
   And claps immortal wings.

He plucks the fruit from life's fair tree
  With yon enraptured throng,
And boundless love shall ever be
  The burden of his song.

Each blazing seraph bold he greets
  And kindles at the sight—
Those jasper walls and golden streets,
  All flame with glory bright.

THE SCHOOL-BOYS' HOLIDAY.

THE school-boys assembled one beautiful day,
    When lessons and labor were ended,
To engage as was meet in some innocent play,
    And to talk of a ramble intended.

Their spirits were joyous, their hearts light and gay,
    Oh, what an unspeakable treasure;
To-morrow, they said, we shall have holiday,
    A time of rejoicing and pleasure.

We will haste to the meadows and forage all over,
    'Neath a green shady tree rest at noon;
We will gather the daisies and pluck the red clover,
    Midst the solace of beauty and bloom.

Next day they arose with the larks at the dawn,
    And their toilets they hastily made,
For at nine of the clock they would wish to be gone,
    And their plans for the future they laid.

The robin sang blithe to his mate in the bush,
    With the music their hearts were in tune;
Then, hurrah for the fields, with a cheer and a rush,
    And there they arrive very soon.

Here they skipped and they played, and somersaults
      made,
    On the side of the hill, warm and sunny,
And they lingered some hours near the sweet-scented
      flowers,
    From which bees were extracting the honey.

They spread a fair cloth where the basket was put
    With the good things they had in possession,
Then of bread and fresh butter, and cheese nicely cut,
    They partook, after asking a blessing.

Next down to the river they cheerily went,
    Where Will caught a fish with a hook;
And Sammy and Percy, with loving consent,
    Took it home to their mother to cook.

When the bright sun was setting they slowly returned,
    All their scenes and adventures relating;
But the poultry were fed, and the milk had been
      churned,
    And their relatives anxiously waiting.

When they reached Maple Grove by the tall iron gate
  They were objects of special attention,
And were tenderly welcomed, though coming so late,
  By the parents and friends at the mansion.

When they entered they heard the sweet voice of a
      singer,
  It came from the drawing-room handsome,
Where a lady pianist, with dainty white fingers,
  Was playing the National Anthem.

One elegant vase held a royal red rose,
  And one a stately white lily,
The fairest in green-house or garden that blows,—
  They were emblems of Rupert and Milly.

Soon to tea they sat down, had a slice of nice cake,
  And cream with ripe strawberries blended;
They had gingerbread, too, and some patties well baked,
  And thus the bright holiday ended.

THE YOUNG MAN OF EXCELLENCE.

WRITTEN BY REQUEST.

YOUNG man of might and noble mind,
　Of marked and true devotion,
Your footprints in the sands of time
　Shall lead to true promotion.

The path of duty still pursue,
　E'en though the tempter whispers;
And joy and peace shall be with you,
　Those loved and lovely sisters.

Should heaven fill your garners wide,
　And bless your house with plenty;
Then be content, nor seek a bride
　Before the age of twenty.

The man whose heart is free from guile
　Is potent to withstand it;
He rears a monumental pile,
　More durable than granite.

Life is a warfare—you must fight,
  Or be a conquered craven ;
But truth and right shall put to flight
  The armies of the alien.

Ye soldiers in this blessed strife,
  Recruits and veterans hoary,
Now marching to the brink of life
  And to the crown of glory :

To God and to your country true,
  With heart as brave as tender,
Upraise the weak and fallen, too,
  And be their sure defender.

Thus all your days may you be found,
  And when complete the number,
And kindly hands have laid you down
  In calm and peaceful slumber ;

The world your honored name shall bless
  When low your head reposes ;
Your memory shall be as the breath
  Of June's first opening roses.

THE COQUETTE.

THE flush of pride was on her cheek,
    Unsteady was her eye;
Her will was strong, her virtues weak,
    And thus she flaunted by.

So like the painted butterfly
    That roams from flower to flower,
And charms the idle passer-by,
    Or loiters in the bower.

When meeting one on duty bound,
    Whose worth she knew full well;
Coquettishly she turned around,
    Her heartless tale to tell.

She said, "I'm out for promenade,
    From care and duty free,
The world was for enjoyment made,
    Then come along with me.

"I've bought a set of jewels rare
    On purpose for the ball,
And necklace that will flash and flare,
    The brightest of them all.

" I've suit of silk, as shall be seen,
    'Tis neither black nor brown,
But changeful like the peacock green,
    The nicest in the town.

" I've costly dresses, eight or nine,
    And flowers of brilliant hue ;
My wardrobe all is passing fine,
    I mean to travel too.

" My hat is of the richest sheen,
    With feather long and gay ;
And life is one delightful dream,
    This happy summer day.

" Of late my father looks so ill
    And casts sad eyes on me ;
But when he dies I'll roam at will,
    Perchance will cross the sea."

The one addressed, though silent erst,
    With pity then replied,
" Permit me now to counsel you,
    And be your friend and guide.

" Whom would you most desire to please
    With ornaments so fine,
Fair goddess of the devotees
    That worship at your shrine ?

" The perfumed puff, with maudlin mind,
　　And heart as hard as steel,
Who is a burden to mankind,
　　As every one must feel ;

" Whose hair is parted like a maid's,
　　Well oiled and pasted down,
Or twisted in fantastic curve,
　　Befitting to a clown ?

" With ladies in the ambulance,
　　He always aims to sit,
Although he is devoid at once,
　　Of manners and of wit.

" A hat is perfect in its sort,
　　As any in the town,
Of straw, or chip, as shall comport
　　With mantle, and with gown.

" The color, if a quiet one,
　　Need not be always brown ;
But wear a plain and silken band,
　　To tie your bonnet down.

" Those jewels, let them hence be cast,
　　Or sink into the flood,
Extorted from a father's woes,
　　They are the price of blood.

" While fashion is a cruel thing,
　　There's much expense incurred,
　And feathers pluck'd from out the wing
　　Of many a beauteous bird.

" This restless tide shall bear you on
　　To a dark and dismal goal,
　It drowns the fortune, wrecks the home,
　　And ruins many a soul.

" Escape the idle and profane
　　Who seek your overthrow,
　Whose life a record is of shame,
　　Of misery and woe.

" The roe is fleeing from its fate,
　　Before the hunter's quiver ;
　A moment more would be too late,
　　It 'scapes it now or never.

" And thus may you escape the snare
　　That threatens to destroy
　Your name, your heritage, your all,
　　Of earthly, heavenly joy.

" Oh, turn and walk in wisdom's ways,
　　She will to you unfold
　Her priceless treasure, length of days,
　　More precious far than gold."

TO MY DAUGHTER, ON HER APPROACHING MARRIAGE.

WE'VE journeyed in the vale of time
    For many a year together;
We've loved and cherished the sublime
    Through fair and stormy weather.

When others were on pleasure bent,
    And vainly sought alliance,
You struggled up in steep ascent,
    That leads to art and science.

But now you go with joy and mirth,
    And steps that will not falter,
To plight your love and faith till death
    Before the bridal altar.

The greatest bliss that heaven supplies
    Be yours and his forever;
And may the current of your lives
    Be like a placid river.

5

.When duty calls you to attend,
  Or roam the wide world over,
You'll have a true and constant friend
  In him, your manly lover.

And when you take the solemn vow,
  From him no more to sever,
If laurels wither on your brow,
  Let love be green forever.

TO MY DEAR AND ESTIMABLE COUSIN,
MISS E. BLAIR,

I SAW thee young and beautiful
  In life's enchanting morn,
As when the rising sun foretells
  A day without a storm,
The loved, the excellent; beside
Thou wert thy mother's joy and pride.

And beautiful thy life hath been,
  Thou generous heart and true,
Who lived for others more than self,
  Though few have lived for you.
'Tis thus with minds of heavenly mould,
Of priceless worth, unsung, untold.

Still bright the lustre of thine eye,
  Though youth has passed away,
And hope and love that cannot die
  Are verdant as the bay.

Empires may wane and be forgot,
But faith and hope shall perish not.

The grace of noble womanhood
   Adorns thee like a crown,
Few were thy peers in all the years,
   'Neath fortune's smile or frown.
O virgin wise! O matron true!
We gladly give the palm to you.

We seldom meet, except in dreams,
   To tell our hopes and fears;
For life is fraught with many a change,
   Alternate smiles and tears:
Yet thought can travel fast and far
When you become its guiding star.

I think of thee at early morn,
   And oft you seem so nigh;
I think of thee at golden eve
   When zephyrs wander by;
And many a tender greeting send,
On ærial wings, to you, my friend.

My gentle cousin, ever dear,
   Whate'er our lot may be,
When heaven is gained, 'twill matter not
   We've sailed a stormy sea:
Laurels are fitly worn by few,
But let me twine a wreath for you.

Until this brow is marble cold,
  This throbbing heart at rest,
Thy name shall ever be enrolled
  The brightest and the best ;
Thy treasured name I will inscribe
On memory's page, there to abide.

We'll often think of summer land,
  Where angel-footsteps stray,
All radiant in their snowy bands,
  They hail us on our way ;
There may our kindred one and all
Assemble at the muster call.

'Twere sweeter than Æolian harp
  To hear thy voice again,
Whose music has inspired me oft
  In pleasure or in pain.
Accept this wreath of fading flowers,
Till crowned with life in Eden's bowers.

IN MEMORIAM.

AH! sweetest rosebud, opening fair,
　So rudely snatched by death from us;
This one memento—lock of hair—
　Thy mother's hands have braided thus.

And hath thy gentle spirit flown
　To summer skies, unswept by storms—
Another jewel for the crown
　Of Him who wore the crown of thorns?

And dost thou shine a glorious star
　Above thy friends and kindred dear;
From earth and time removed so far,
　If heaven be far and yet so near?

I saw thee once, fair opening rose,
　Too fragile for the coming storm;
And warmly did my heart enclose
　A transient joy but newly born.

When sinks the mortal frame oppress'd,
　Ere life's departing ray hath fled,
There is a place—'tis Jesus' breast—
　On which to rest the dying head.

The glorious light of heaven, serene,
   Where spirits pure shall e'er exist;
Beyond death's dark and sullen stream,
   We dimly see as through a mist.

Beyond the reach of mortal fears,
   No troublous wave thy rest shall mar;
Beyond the reach of sin and tears,
   To be with Christ is better far.

No dark'ning shadows interpose
   To dim thy bright, unclouded sun;
Rest from the strife of human woes,
   The cross is past, the crown is won.

Come, sisters, let us take some flowers
   To scatter on her early grave;
Of such as grow in shady bowers,
   Where purest, sweetest blossoms wave.

Bring fragrant roses, fresh and fair,
   And modest lily of the vale,
With morning glory here and there,
   And jessamine, so sweet and pale.

Bring daisies, pluck'd from off the sod,—
   Emblems of innocence are they;
We see them smiling up to God
   Beside our path on life's rough way.

Bring pansies of the velvet eye,
 As blue, as purple as the sky ;
And violets we love so dear—
 These humble flowers are welcome here.

These fitting emblems now we clasp,
 And gently on her bosom lay ;
Like her, too beautiful to last,
 Whose life was but a summer day.

And shall not angels see them there,
 Bending to view them from above,
Our human sympathy to share,
 Partakers of a kindred love?

SUSAN BLYTHE.

WHEN fiction is by fancy led,
　　It roams where'er it will ;
But has it not been truly said
　　That facts are stranger still ?

Sweet Susan Blythe was early left
　　To share a stranger's home,
Of parents fond and true bereft
　　Who lived at Aldercombe.

Her father was an officer,
　　Both honored and renowned,
And chivalrous as any knight
　　That trod on battle-ground.

Her mother was a lady fair,
　　Both gentle and refined,
Who was endowed with talents rare,
　　Possess'd of noble mind.

Her husband as a hero fell,
   But left an honored name;
She followed soon; their only child
   An orphan then became.

The child was sent to cottage home,
   Not far from Hazel Grove;
The woodbine clustered round its walls,
   That home of peace and love.

Here, soon a lovely girl she grew,
   And early in her youth
She read the blessed Bible through,
   And prized its sacred truth.

To many a child of woe and want,
   She ministered in love;
She seemed like some fair visitant
   Sent from the throne above.

Dear, gentle Susan, oft was she
   Among the garden bowers,
Where humming-bird and busy bee
   Beguiled the fleeting hours.

The fairest of them all she stands
   In beauty half divine;
The while she trains with careful hands
   The myrtle and the vine.

She had a sweet, impressive face,
    An eye of finest mould ;
Her silken hair flowed to the waist
    In waves of living gold.

One eve, as she was walking there,
    Fann'd by the zephyrs mild,
A nobleman approached the fair,
    Who raised his hat and smiled.

On summer evenings oft of late
    He pass'd the flow'ry cot;
He sometimes chanced to rusticate
    Near this sequestered spot.

He rode hard by the garden gate,
    Then drew the bridle-rein,
'Twas evident he wished to speak
    On some important theme.

She knew not of his vast estate,—
    She knew not of his name ;
But quick discerned that he was mate
    To fortune and to fame.

She met his glance with half a smile,
    She bow'd as her became ;
But conversation waived the while
    Until he should explain.

He said, "I've walked baronial halls,
    And green Arcadian bowers,
But would enjoy much more than all,
    A walk among your flowers.

"Their perfume is so sweet," he said,
    " And rich their varied sheen ;
Here beauties rare their petals spread,
    But 'mongst them you are queen."

She blushed, and turning half around
    To hide her crimson cheek,
She answered in a voice profound,
    But yet divinely meek,

"Why flatter me, because alone
    The rose is queen of flowers ;
But soon its beauty shall be gone,
    A fitting type of ours.

"With pleasure, I will show you all
    Our pleasant garden through,
And pluck the flower you like the best,
    Whate'er its name or hue.

"Will you accept this rose," she said,
    "This queenly scented blossom ?"
He took the rose of royal red
    And placed it in his bosom ;

Saying, "Thank you, miss," and bowing low,
    " This is an emblem meet
Of beauty and perfection too,
    In all its parts complete.

" Its loveliness is not excelled
    By any flower that blows;
Castellan vase has never held
    So sweet, so fine a rose.

" For your dear sake, I'll wear it in
    The place that love assigns it;
Will you accept my diamond ring?"
    She modestly declines it.

He frankly said, ere he withdrew
    From that Elysian spot,
" This one request I ask of you,
    Dear miss, forget me not."

Then turning round as quick as thought,
    His saddle to regain ;
He rode a charger lately brought
    From Portugal or Spain.

Time passed—among the flowers she stood,
    Still beauteous as before,
When lo, a livery servant stood
    Outside the cottage door.

He rapped a hasty rap, and soon
  The door wide open flew,
" A letter for Miss Blythe," he said,
  Then promptly he withdrew.

She sought her chamber to unfold,
  And read this letter bland ;
Mountmorris offered her his gold,
  And offered her his hand.

His future bliss he would confide
  To her so young and fair ;
He asked her to become his bride,
  And tell him when and where.

She answered soon to his address,
  " Mountmorris, number three ;"
Her style is graphic, clear and terse,
  As we shall shortly see.

" My lord, the question you advance
  Has most perplexing been ;   ·
'Tis like a legend of romance,
  Or like a passing dream.

" To accept your hand my humble lot
  Forbids me to aspire ;
Your wealth, your gold, I prize it not,
  Nor do I it desire.

" On fancy's wing I may not soar
So high as Castle Green,
Whose frescoed walls and folding doors
Befit no humble mien.

" The rich and poor commingle not,
Until this life is past;
But then they share a common lot,
A kindred home at last.

" Forgive, if error is in me,
I wish not to offend;
I have the honor thus to be
Respectfully, your friend."

This note was in the office laid
By cousin Sue Vantassel,
And after, duly was conveyed
To him of Greenwood Castle.

He glanced it o'er with silent haste,
And pleased was he to find
Its sober contents closely traced
So strong, so pure a mind.

But was it possible that she
Should still unheeding prove,
When one so dignified as he
Had deigned to ask her love?

Slumber forsook his longing eyes,
  The dove of peace had flown;
Ere long he sought her in disguise,
  And found her all alone.

His guiding star has led to her
  Who is of humble mien,
And love has thrown the barrier down
  That rank had raised between.

The introduction here was brief,
  They pleasantly shook hands,
And soon this young romantic chief
  Thus earnestly began:

"Miss Blythe, the contents of your note
  To me have given pain;
If you reject my humble suit,
  All others I disdain."

Her eyelids gently rose and fell,
  Anon she said with calmness,
"Sir, I am but a peasant girl,
  And you are Lord Mountmorris.

"How then should I your equals meet,
  Who tread your stately halls,
With education incomplete,
  And fortune none at all?"

In silvery tones she answered yet,
  "Your Lordship's *fiancee*
With courtly airs and etiquette
  Should well acquainted be."

He quick replied: "My peers are those
  In wisdom who excel;
But not the arrogant, morose,
  Self-constituted swell.

"Your native elegance and worth
  Should still assert their sway,
Should dim the splendors of a court,
  And bear the palm away.

"Now bless me with your hand, my sweet,
  And link your fate to mine;
For truer heart did never beat
  In woman's breast than thine!"

He paused; she smiled a sweet consent,—
  She answered, "Come what may,
For love so true, my heart is yours
  Until my dying day."

Her eyes a peerless lustre shed;
  Her cheek with beauty glows,
The tender maiden bow'd her head
  As bows the virgin rose.

6

He, like a palm-tree, stood erect,
   A happy lover now;
A ring he gave his bride elect,
   And kissed her marble brow.

A parting smile he now bestows,
   Like sunshine after rain; ·
Soon each to each shall plight their vows,
   And never part again.

The earth again had rolled its round,
   Another day was born,
The golden sun was shining down
   To hail that festive morn.

The hum of bees, the songs of birds,
   With music fill'd the air;
The bride was dressed in flowing robes,
   With blossoms in her hair.

The bridegroom early was announced
   With triumph and display;
Then to St. Paul's their course they bent,
   To be made one for aye.

But ere the carriage her receives,
   Which bore her thence away,
A document the post-boy leaves
   Is read without delay.

. . . "they stood within
The old cathedral grand."

Page 84.

The Ministry of Flowers.

This letter was from Anson Burr,
    A legal gentleman;
Officially he wrote to her,
    And thus the contents ran:

" It is my office to relate
    Your uncle's will is found,
And you inherit his estate
    And thirty thousand pounds."

Eight hours elapsed; they stood within
    The old Cathedral grand,—
And lo ! the solemn rites begin,
    The bishop joins their hand.

" May heaven bless them from above !"
    From hill and dale it rings,
And o'er the scene of holy love
    Let angels spread their wings.

The foe that would those hearts divide
    Must sure be Satan's vassal ;
Mountmorris and his blushing bride
    Now leave for Greenwood Castle.

With milder ray the king of day
    On all devotion stamps :
'Tis evening now, and twilight gray
    Hangs out her silver lamps.

She sought communion with the skies,
  A moment even there ;
She gently closed her azure eyes,
  And clasped her hands in prayer.

Her lily cheek begins to glow ;
  She sees the turrets high,
That seem to point in weal or woe
  To joys that never die.

They now arrive at Castle Green,
  Mountmorris and his bride,
Where fragrant flowers of every sheen
  Fling odors far and wide.

Banners are proudly waving here
  Above the ancient walls,
And bright and gorgeous chandeliers
  Light up the festive halls.

A master touch has woke the chords
  That tremble on the lyre,
And bards' and poets' hearts are stirred
  With fresh poetic fire.

They enter, diamonds flash and blaze
  Around the bride serene ;
But all her words and all her ways
  Are worthy of a queen.

He led her through ancestral halls,
  Where sires reclined of old ;
Where hung the richest tapestry,
  Of crimson and of gold.

Mountmorris then his bride did cheer
  With loving words and kind :
He said, "Henceforth, my gentle dear,
  This wealth is yours and mine."

She said, "Our Father in the sky,
  So let Thy will be done
By us on earth as 'tis on high
  By angels round thy throne."

Then to her lord she answered thus,
  " The poor have wants and woes,
And shall they not partake with us
  What bounties heaven bestows ?

" If others lack of daily bread,
  Let us their wants supply ;
So shall our souls be blest and fed
  With manna from on high."

Diviner treasure still she sought—
  Of wisdom, grace and truth—
But ne'er forgot the humble cot
  Or guardian of her youth.

No more this high-souled, gentle wife
   Shall dread a cold world's frown;
Her husband loves her as his life,
   She is his joy and crown.

Their long and happy lives abound
   With blessings, we are told;
And man should always wed for love,
   But never wed for gold.

WINDSOR CASTLE.

ON THE OCCASION OF THE QUEEN'S JUBILEE.

MONARCH serene! beloved Queen!
  Accept an ardent wish from me;
I write for neither praise nor fame
  This humble offering to thee.

They celebrate thy jubilee
  From shore to shore, from sea to sea;
Let others blow the trump of fame,
  I wish God's blessing still for thee.

To sway the sceptre thou wast born,
  Chosen of God and honored thou
The crown thy life hath so adorned,
  Long may it rest upon thy brow

FATE OF THE CAPTIVE BIRDS.

In a branch of a rosy apple tree,
   Canaries built their nest,
And soon a helpless family
   Had come to be caressed.

The eastern sky was all aglow,
   The sun did cheer and strengthen;
The mother whispered, bending low,
   "My darlings, you are welcome!"

Theirs was a pretty rounded nest,
   Neatly and well combined;
And all with wool and thistle-down,
   So softly it was lined.

The parents gathered food by day,
   Where tiny insects float;
And gladly brought the treasured prey
   To fill each gaping throat.

They soon return with needful food,
　Nor would their stay prolong;
But who shall tell what grief befell
　To find their offspring gone?

Rude hands had torn the nest away,
　With birdies one and all,
And placed it in a grim old cage
　That hung against the wall.

The parent birds sad fate bemoan,
　But pity them inspires
To feed their young, their hapless own,
　Through the cold unyielding wires.

For there, with direst grief oppressed,
　The young ones chirping lay;
No sheltering wing or mother's breast
　To warm them night or day.

O'ercome at length with grief and fear,
　They laid them down to die;
And who that ever shed a tear,
　Could look with tearless eye?

A caged bird is a piteous thing,
　Then let the captive fly;
Nor seek to tame the dauntless wing
　That soars to meet the sky.

For it is cruelty and sin,
 Though practised everywhere,
To take God's birds and shut them in
 To sorrow and despair.

Oh, fie on those who would engage
 To spoil a life of song!
The prison that we call a cage,
 To them is cruel wrong.

THE LOST CHILD.

ONE morn in September, a child two years old
  From the cottage had wandered away;
So tiny and small was the dear little doll,
  She could hide in a bundle of hay.

The narrow path led from the house to the wood,
  Where sauntered the wild beasts of prey;
Soon the innocent child disappeared in the wild,
  Lost, lost as it seemed for aye.

The mother ran wild in the search for her child,
  But the baby could nowhere be found;
Then tidings were spread of a child lost or dead,
  And the neighbors were summoned around.

They sought her amain, but they sought her in vain,
  Though her steps for a time they could trace;
But the footprints were gone, which had guided them
    on
  Till she passed from the sand to the grass.

Away through the forest she's wandering on,
  Till night with its darkness surround her ;
And she hears 'neath the pines like the sound of the
      sea,
  But the angels are watching around her.

Night ended the search, till the dawn of next day,
  The disconsolate parents are weeping ;
For Louisa is cold on the hills far away,
  But the angels their vigil are keeping.

Her delicate form of a covering was void,
  Save a hat and a gossamer dress ;
If the night had been frosty the child must have died
  In the arms of that lone wilderness.

Next morning they sought her in vain as before ;
  Still no trace of the long-missing child,
Till darkness was mantling the forest once more,
  And then she emerged from the wild.

Near the edge of a clearance she wandered about,
  For the angels had guided her there ;
O bliss without measure ! O joy beyond doubt !
  For the hearts she had left in despair.

There they found the lost child with the hat in her
    hand
  That erst she had worn on her head ;
But affrighted she gazed, for her eyes they were dazed,
  Of her dress there was only a shred.

Then they carried her back from that wilderness wide
  To the mother, forlorn and distress'd ;
But the joy of that mother no tongue can describe,
  When her child to her bosom she pressed.

AUNT PHŒBE'S STORY.

I ENTERED a neat little cottage
  One eve in the bright summer time;
Aunt Phœbe was reading the Bible,
  Her look was serene and benign.

I asked of her welfare, she answered,
  "Our garments are threadbare and thin,
But riches, my Father in heaven,
  My trust is all centered in Him.

"Our Katie is gone with the angels,
  And we are grown old, as you see;
And cold are the shadows of evening,
  Which gather round Jacob and me.

"But closer we cleave to each other,
  Our hearts are still tender and warm,
We walk in the sunshine together,
  Together we battle the storm.

"Dear Katie, before she departed,
  Exclaimed, with a smile on her face,
' O mother! the angels are coming,
  I go to a happier place.

"' When all your rough voyage is o'er, mother,
  Together we'll sing the new song;
I will linger awhile on the shore, mother,
  For I know you will join me ere long.'

" And then the bright eyes of our darling
  Began to grow misty and dim,
And she kissed me good-bye in the morning,
  Ere Jesus had called her to Him.

" They bore her to her resting-place
  With solemn tread and slow;
The old church bell rang out the knell,
  The sun was sinking low.

" And there, beneath the emerald sod,
  We laid her down to rest;
Nor murmured at the will of God;
  What He ordains is best.

" We gathered round the hearth once more,
  But now it seems so lone;
The easy chair was vacant there,
  Our sweetest bird had flown.

7

"The hymn she loved, our gentle dove,
    We read with tearful eyes ;
  Come, let us join our friends above,
    That have obtained the prize.

"But still she is round me and near me,
    I feel it when nobody knows ;
  I see her sweet smile in the daisy,
    Her innocent blush in the rose.

"She whispers, 'Dear mother, be faithful,
    For time's growing shorter, you see,
  And when you get home to the bright land,
    I've the sweetest of welcomes for thee.'"

OUR LITTLE HATTIE,

WHO DIED MARCH 29TH, 18__ AD 6 YEARS AND 10 MONTHS.

" He shall gather the lamb."

SHE bow'd ; the messenger had come
    Each earthly tie to sever ;
The King Immortal took her home
    To be with Him forever.

She droop'd like a wilted flower
    Untimely frosts have smitten ;
But the name we gave when she was ours
    In the Book of Life is written.

The lips that smiled the rosy smile,
    That talked and laughed so freely,
Lisp slowly now in accents mild,
    " Mother, I cannot see thee."

She trembles in the cold embrace
    Of death's relentless river ;
But hark ! her spirit rests in peace
    Forever and forever.

Above the cold and lifeless clay,
　　With angels now ascending,
She enters the courts of perfect day,
　　And glory never ending.

Like Noah's dove of weary wing,
　　She's reached the ark at last ;
But who shall tell the change between
　　The present and the past ?

And soon we laid the little frame
　　Down in the earth's cold bosom ;
But 'twas a guardian angel came
　　And pluck'd the tender blossom.

The broken casket empty lies
　　Till resurrection morning,
When they who sleep in Christ shall rise
　　With joy at His returning.

The gentle Hattie, heir of bliss,
　　Is from our household taken ;
Long shall we miss the good-night kiss,
　　Cast down, but not forsaken.

O Thou supreme and loving Lord !
　　To Thee our all we offer ;
Thy righteous will by heaven adored
　　Help us to do and suffer.

THE OUTLOOK.

WE'RE hurrying on to fairer skies,
    Away from winter's chill ;
And faith exults to see the prize
    Nearer, yet nearer still.

We catch the breath of sweet perfume
    From glory fields afar ;
Celestial light shines through the gloom,
    The bright and morning star.

We dash the tear-drops from our eyes,
    And from this rugged strand
We sight the hills of Paradise,
    Our dear Immanuel's land.

Sweet Promised Land of heavenly rest !
    Hither the tribes shall come ;
From north and south, from east and west,
    And all unite as one.

They signal us from over there—
  Companions, children, friends—
Then let us haste away to live
  The life that never ends.

At evening time there shall be light,
  The light of faith and love,
More beautiful, serene and bright,
  Allied to heaven above.

We ask each day that daily bread
  And needful grace be given,
To follow Christ, our living Head,
  To victory and to heaven.

SOLOMA'S DREAM.

Soloma loved to watch the surf,
   As it broke on the sea-beat shore,
And lightly she bounded o'er the turf
   At the splash of the boatman's oar.

She chased the corncrake through the corn,
   With eager, childish glee;
She hung a burdock on a thorn,
   And weighed the dust for tea.

Beside the hedge she wandered lone,
   Or sported on the green;
She climbed the stile,—it was a throne,
   And she a fairy queen.

And here, on the margin of the brook,
   O'erhung with reeds and ferns,
She learned to study nature's book,
   Her beauties to discern.

And here, on a verdant bank reclined,
   Beside a crystal stream,
She found the magnet of the mind,
   She dreamt her childhood's dream.

Was it a dream ? the dream was this,—
   Or inspiration given,
Of future woe, of future bliss,
   Of sorrow, joy and heaven ?

Again she waded in the brook,
   But shadows fell thereon,
And dark and cold the waters rolled,
   A river deep and strong.

The moon looked down with shimmering ray,
   The light of day had fled ;
Earth seemed a battle-field, where lay
   The dying and the dead.

An eager crowd was pressing on,
   In a broad and open way ;
The drunkard sang his ribald song
   Or bacchanalian lay.

And round her raved incarnate fiends
   Of fury and of sin ;
She sought the river to escape,
   They pushed her farther in.

The scene is changed, an angel form
    Is sweetly bending o'er;
She dreads not now the threatening storm,
    But steps upon the shore.

She dreamt of mother at her side,
    To bless her tender years;
To check or guide the rushing tide
    Of childhood's hopes and fears.

She heard celestial music roll,
    And sweetest numbers play,
Which left its impress on her soul,
    Ere yet it died away.

Flute, viola, diapason,
    Tremulant, seraphone,
Voice melodia, voice celeste,
    Treble and bass intone.

And here she found a lovely harp,
    To her it did belong;
Her heart's deep lore henceforth to pour
    In melody and song.

Her slumbers broke, and then she woke
    Smiling amidst her tears;
Her sunny curls the mother stroked,
    And soothed her childish fears.

SHEPHERDS OF THE EAST.

Now shepherds were since time began
    Men of immortal fame;
The first was Eve's devoted son,
    And Abel was his name.

The simple pastoral he sung
    Rose on the air sublime;
He led his flocks the hills among,
    In that primeval time.

Moses was once a shepherd in
    The land of Midian;
Twas there he saw the burning bush,
    Where God appeared to him.

And Jesse's son, a shepherd young,
    Was Israel's pride and joy;
He tuned his harp to sacred song,
    When but a shepherd boy.

They spoke his name with loud acclaim,
  And maids were wont to sing
Of David when a shepherd boy,
  Of David when a king.

To humble shepherds angels came
  By night at Bethlehem,
Messiah's advent to proclaim,
  " Peace and good-will to men."

BEULAH.

IT is the border-land of heaven,
  The dawn of endless day,
Where joyful antepast is given
  Of perfect bliss for aye.

It is a region of delight
  Where heavenly watchers stray;
The air is warm, the sun shines bright
  With mild, celestial ray.

Here rests the Christian for a time
  Beneath supernal bowers;
The wilderness is left behind
  For Eden's fruits and flowers.

He feasts on heavenly manna here,
  It may be for a day:
A whisper speaks the Bridegroom near,
  Nor tarry long he may.

Homeward he turns his longing eyes,
   And hope his spirit fills,
For just across the river rise
   The everlasting hills.

Hope lifts the timid spirit up
   To look within the vale;
Faith leans on hope, celestial hope,
   Whose anchor cannot fail.

He sees a land to death unknown,
   A pure and happy clime,
Where saints and seraphs round the throne
   In bright effulgence shine.

Thou glorious New Jerusalem,
   Bright city of our King,
The tearless eye shall look on thee
   Where glad hosannas ring.

He sees heaven's smile on every face,
   Heaven's light in every eye;
The shining form, the saintly grace,
   Of beauty throned on high.

He hears the ransomed children sing
   In concert round the throne;
From death's domain the heavenly King
   Hath claimed them for his own.

Sweet birds of Paradise, ye won
　　The goal at early morn,
And like the lark, that seeks the sun,
　　Ye soared above the storm.

He sees the glad immortal eyes
　　With softest radiance beam,
The balmy groves of Paradise,
　　With flowery vales between.

But oh! he sees the Saviour, dear,
　　So full of truth and grace,
That every wanderer may draw near,
　　And rest in his embrace.

www.ingramcontent.com/pod-product-compliance
Lightning Source LLC
Chambersburg PA
CBHW020806020726
47495CB00008B/2618